$7.95

I WISH LAURA'S MOMMY WAS MY MOMMY

by Barbara Power

Pictures by Marylin Hafner

Jennifer liked Laura's mother very much. In fact, sometimes she wished Laura's mommy was *her* mommy. But then everything changed. Jennifer's mother went back to work, and Laura's mother babysat for Jennifer and her brothers. And Jennifer had to take a new look at both mothers.

The humorous illustrations in this book for beginning readers show Marylin Hafner's understanding of Jennifer's dilemma.

I WISH LAURA'S MOMMY WAS MY MOMMY

A Lippincott I-Like-To-Read Book

I WISH LAURA'S MOMMY WAS MY MOMMY

by Barbara Power

Pictures by Marylin Hafner

J. B. Lippincott   New York

Library of Congress Cataloging in Publication Data

Power, Barbara.
  I wish Laura's mommy was my mommy.

  (A Lippincott I-like-to-read book)
  SUMMARY: Jennifer thinks she prefers life in
Laura's home to her own until changing circumstances
help her to understand her own mother better.
  [1. Mothers—Fiction.   2. Mothers—Employment—
Fiction]   I. Hafner, Marylin.   II. Title.
PZ7.P8822Iad   [E]   79-2406
ISBN-0-397-31838-3
ISBN-0-397-31859-6 (LB)

FOR ADRIANNE . . . B.P.

FOR NAIAD, ONE OF THE BEST . . . M.H.

Laura and Jennifer were friends. When Jennifer went to Laura's house after school, Laura's mother gave them something good to eat. They had punch and cookies, or donuts, or sometimes even candy.

When Laura came to Jennifer's house, they had fruit or graham crackers. Jennifer's mother said, "Snacks should be real food, not just sugar."

"I wish my mommy had better snacks," thought Jennifer. "I wish she gave us good things like Laura's mommy. I wish Laura's mommy was my mommy."

When Jennifer had dinner at
Laura's house, they all ate in the
dining room. Sometimes they ate by
candlelight.

If the girls wanted more dessert,
Laura's mother got it for them.

After dinner, she would say, "All
right, girls, you may leave the table
and play until it's time for Jennifer to
go home."

Then she would clear the table and do the dishes while Laura's father read the newspaper.

Jennifer's family always ate in the kitchen because her brothers, Joshua and Jeremy, were very messy eaters.

After dinner, Jennifer had to help clear the table. Her mother put the boys to bed and her father put the dishes in the dishwasher. If she wanted more dessert, she had to get it for herself.

Sometimes there wasn't enough dessert for seconds.

"I wish my mommy would clear the table and get me more dessert like Laura's mommy," thought Jennifer. "I wish Laura's mommy was my mommy."

I WISH LAURA'S MOMMY WAS MY MOMMY

One night Jennifer slept over at
Laura's house. The girls played
monster. They laughed until Jennifer
had to go to the bathroom.

Laura's mother came in. She gave
them each a second good-night kiss
and told them to have sweet dreams.

In the morning, Jennifer and Laura played while Laura's mother fixed breakfast. She made pancakes shaped like little people. Jennifer had three.

"I love pancakes," she told Laura's mother.

When Laura slept over at Jennifer's house, Jeremy came in at bedtime. They all had a pillow fight. They tried to giggle as quietly as they could. Joshua started to fuss in his crib.

They went to get him so he could
play with them too. The door banged.
Jennifer's mother came upstairs.
"I want all of you to go back to bed
right now," she said.

In the morning, Jennifer's mother had to change Joshua and help Jeremy get dressed. She told the girls to make the bed and fold the blankets on the cot.

Jennifer's father made coffee and
fixed eggs for himself and Jennifer's
mother. Jennifer and Laura toasted
their own English muffins. Then they
helped themselves to cereal.

"I wish my mommy would make my bed," thought Jennifer. "I wish she would make pancakes shaped like little people the way Laura's mommy does. I wish Laura's mommy was my mommy."

I WISH LAURA'S MOMMY WAS MY MOMMY

One day Jennifer's parents told her
that her mother was going back to work.
Jennifer didn't want her mother to
go back to work. Thinking about it
gave her a funny feeling inside.

"Who will be here when I get home from school?" she asked. "Who will take care of Jeremy and Joshua?"

Jennifer's father said they would
have to think about babysitters.

"I don't want to think about
babysitters!" Jennifer shouted.

But then she had an idea.

"I know," she said. "How about
Laura's mommy? She doesn't go to
work, and she likes us and I like her."

Jennifer's mother called up Laura's
mother.

Laura's mother said she would
like to babysit for Jennifer and
Jeremy and Joshua.

"Neato," thought Jennifer.

When Jennifer went home with
Laura after school on Monday, Laura's
mother gave them punch
and donuts.

Jeremy and Joshua came into the kitchen. They wanted punch and donuts too. Laura's mother poured them some punch and gave them each half a donut.

"Goodness, I'd forgotten how it is with little ones," she said. "Now they won't eat any dinner."

The next day after school, Laura's mother gave them apples.

"Could I have a donut?" asked Jennifer.

"I'm sorry, Jennifer," said Laura's mother. "Donuts are fine for a treat once in a while, but fruit is much better for you."

On Wednesday after school, Laura's mother asked Jennifer to show Laura how to make her bed.

"Your mother told me that you make your bed every morning. I think Laura should learn to do hers too," she said.

Laura didn't want to learn how to make her bed. "I don't see why I have to," she told her mother.

"I have much more to do around the house with Jennifer and the boys here every day," said Laura's mother. "You're old enough to do a few things for yourself."

So Jennifer showed Laura how to make her bed. Laura didn't do it nearly as well as Jennifer did.

The next night, Jennifer's mother had to work late. Jennifer, Jeremy, and Joshua had dinner at Laura's. They all ate in the kitchen. Jennifer couldn't believe it.

Laura's father said he liked to eat in
the kitchen the way they had when
Laura was little.

"Could we have candlelight?" asked Jennifer.

"I'm sorry, Jennifer," said Laura's mother. "The boys are too little. They would pay more attention to the candles than to their food."

After dinner, Laura's father told
Laura and Jennifer to clear the table
so he could clean up the kitchen while
Laura's mother cleaned up Jeremy
and Joshua.

Laura didn't know how to scrape
and stack the plates.

On Friday night, Jennifer's parents took her and her brothers out to dinner. They went to a pizza place and had pizza with pepperoni. Jennifer loved pepperoni.

41

On Saturday, Jennifer's mother asked her if she wanted to help bake a cake.

"Neato! Can we make a chocolate cake?" asked Jennifer.

While Jeremy and Joshua were having their nap, Jennifer and her mother baked the cake. Jennifer cracked the eggs and sifted the flour with the cocoa.

She told her mother what had happened at school during the week. Her mother told her about the office and what she did there.

She invited Jennifer to come and see her office one day when school had let out for the summer.

They made pink frosting for the
cake. Jennifer's mother said, "You lick
the bowl, Pumpkin Princess," the way
she had when Jennifer was little.
Jennifer felt warm and happy.

"I still like Laura's mommy," she
thought, "but I'm glad my mommy is
my mommy."

About the Author

Barbara Power has worked as a newspaper reporter, a social worker, a teacher, and an editor. She lives in West Trenton, New Jersey, with her husband and two children. *I Wish Laura's Mommy Was My Mommy* is her first book.

About the Artist

Marylin Hafner's illustrations have appeared in seventeen books for children and in numerous magazines. Ms. Hafner is also a sculptor. She has three daughters and lives in Cambridge, Massachusetts.